SPONGEBOB SQUAREPANTS

SPONGEBOB'S EASTER PARADE

By Steven Banks
Cover illustrated by Heather Martinez
Interior illustrated by Barry Goldberg

A Random House PICTUREBACK® Book

Random House 🏠 New York

created by

Stephen Hillenburg

randomhouse.com/kids
ISBN: 978-0-449-81444-4
Printed in the United States of America
10 9 8 7 6 5 4 3 2 1

The streets of Bikini Bottom were empty!

"Oh, no!" cried Patrick. "We're the only two people left!"

SpongeBob laughed. "No, Patrick," he said. "Everybody's at home working on their floats for the Easter Parade so they can win the Golden Egg Award!"

"Is our float done?" asked Patrick.

"We haven't even started it," said SpongeBob. "Remember? We went jellyfishing and bubble watching and we had a burp contest and you counted all my holes."

"That was fun!" shouted Patrick. "Let's do it again!" SpongeBob shook his head. "No, Patrick, we gotta start working on our Easter float!"

SpongeBob and Patrick ran home.

Squidward was coming out of his house. "How's your Easter float coming?" he asked. "I bet you two goof-offs haven't even started!"

"Wrong!" said Patrick. "We haven't even thought about it!"

Squidward laughed. "Good luck!" he called as he went back inside. "The parade's tomorrow morning!"

"We can do it!" announced SpongeBob.

"Let's put witches and ghosts on it!" Patrick suggested.

"It's not Halloween," said SpongeBob.

Patrick smiled. "Then let's put Santa Claus and snow on it!"

"It's not Christmas," said SpongeBob.

"Turkeys and pilgrims?" asked Patrick.

"Patrick! It's Easter! Not Thanksgiving!" said SpongeBob.

"An Easter float should have a bunny or Easter eggs," explained SpongeBob.

Patrick picked up an egg, glued it to a piece of wood, and tied a rope to it. "It's done!" he shouted. "We're going to win!"

SpongeBob shook his head. "I don't think so. Let's go look at the other floats."

Patrick and SpongeBob peeked in at Mr. Krabs's float, which featured his daughter, Pearl.

"Argh!" said Mr. Krabs. "This will win the Golden Egg Award and sell Krabby Patties, too!"

Next they spied on Plankton's float, which was just a giant statue of . . . Plankton!

"I have outdone myself!" shouted Plankton. "All will bow down to me as master of the universe when I win the Golden Egg Award! Ha! Ha! Ha!"

Sandy Cheeks had just finished her float when SpongeBob and Patrick peeked in. Sandy looked at her float proudly and said, "This is gonna be the biggest rootin' tootin' float this town has ever seen!"

Squidward's float had Squidward playing his clarinet inside a giant egg.

"I wonder where I should put the Golden Egg Award when I win tomorrow," he said. "I can't wait to see SpongeBob's and Patrick's float. I could use a good laugh!"

"Everybody's floats are better than ours! We'll never win!"
cried SpongeBob. "We shouldn't have gone jellyfishing and
bubble watching and burping!"
"I blame the jellyfish!" said Patrick.

Just then, a truck carrying a beautiful Easter float pulled up.
"Where's Far Reef?" asked the driver. "I gotta deliver this float for
their Easter parade."

SpongeBob pointed down the road. As the truck drove away, it
hit a bump in the road and the float fell off!

SpongeBob ran after the truck. "Hey! Mister Truck Driver!" he
called. "You dropped your float!"

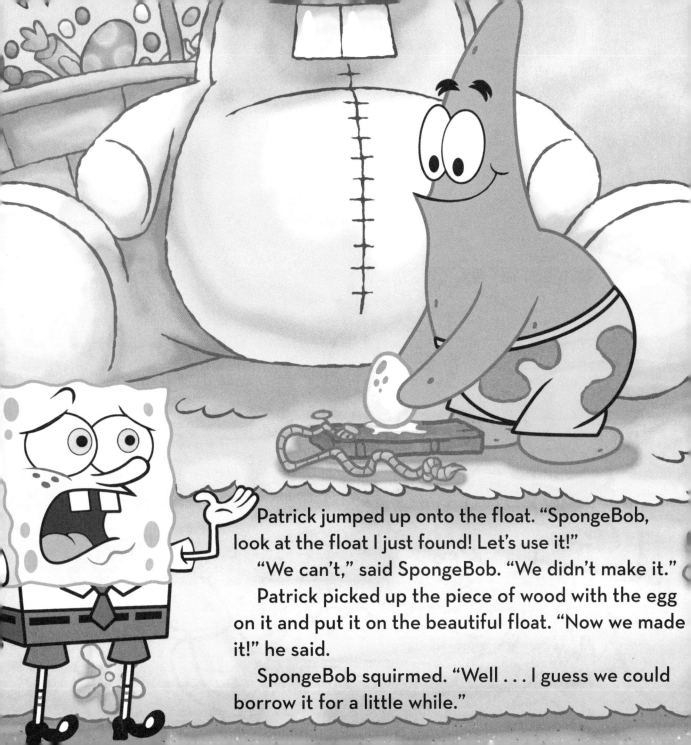

Patrick jumped up onto the float. "SpongeBob, look at the float I just found! Let's use it!"

"We can't," said SpongeBob. "We didn't make it."

Patrick picked up the piece of wood with the egg on it and put it on the beautiful float. "Now we made it!" he said.

SpongeBob squirmed. "Well . . . I guess we could borrow it for a little while."

The next morning, SpongeBob and Patrick showed up with the float.

"That's one heck of a float!" said Sandy.

"It must have cost a pretty penny!" said Mr. Krabs.

"How did you make that so fast?" asked a suspicious Squidward.

"Computers," said Patrick.

The mayor of Bikini Bottom gave SpongeBob and Patrick the Golden Egg Award. "This is the most beautiful Easter float we have ever seen!" he said. "You should be proud!"

SpongeBob tried to smile. "Uh, yeah, we're very proud."

The parade began, and SpongeBob and Patrick's float was right at the front. Everyone was clapping and chanting, "SpongeBob and Patrick! SpongeBob and Patrick!"

Even though everyone was cheering for them, SpongeBob felt bad. He knew they didn't deserve to win.

"STOP THE PARADE!" shouted SpongeBob. "I have a confession. We didn't make this float!"

"We didn't?" asked Patrick.
"It fell off a truck," said SpongeBob.
"We wanted to win the trophy so badly that we cheated."

Plankton stamped his tiny foot.
"Why didn't *I* think of that?"

The Golden Egg Award was divided into four pieces and shared by Sandy, Squidward, Mr. Krabs, and Plankton.

The truck driver returned to pick up his float. "I *thought* I was missing something!" he said.

"Here's the float we made," said SpongeBob.
Sandy laughed. "It's just an egg on a piece of wood!" she said.
"That's the worst Easter float I've ever seen!" said Squidward.
"Yes, it is!" said SpongeBob proudly. "And we made it all by ourselves!"

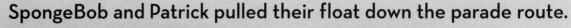

SpongeBob and Patrick pulled their float down the parade route.

"Don't you feel better, Patrick, using our own float?" asked SpongeBob.

"Yeah," said Patrick. "Especially after eating that egg."

"Patrick! You just ate our float!" protested SpongeBob.

"What float?" asked Patrick.

"Never mind," said SpongeBob. "Happy Easter!"